ISBN 1 85854 282 0
© Brimax Books Ltd. 1997. All rights reserved.
Published by Brimax Books Ltd, Newmarket, England, CB8 7AU, 1997.
Printed in France.

Once Upon a Time

Illustrated by Gill Guile

Brimax · Newmarket · England

The Ugly Duckling

Mother Duck has five new ducklings. She has one egg left to hatch. All the birds on the farm come to look at the egg.

"It is too big to be a duck's egg," says a chicken.

"It's a turkey's egg," says a goose.

"How will I know if the baby is a turkey?" asks mother duck.

"It will not swim," says the goose.

At last the egg hatches. The baby that steps out does not look like his brothers and sisters. But he goes straight to the pond for a swim. "You are not a turkey!" says mother duck. But the chickens and geese laugh and say, "What an ugly duckling!"

The little duckling is unhappy. Everyone laughs at him. He decides to run away. The little duckling goes to live by a big lake. One day he sees some wild ducks. "Will you be my friends?" he asks.

But the ducks say, "What an ugly duckling!" They chase him away.

One day, the little duckling sees some swans flying across the sky. "I wish I was a swan. They are very beautiful. No one laughs at them," he says. Winter comes, and it is very cold. Now the little duckling is not only lonely – he is cold and hungry, too.

One night, the lake freezes over. The little duckling's feet are stuck in the ice. The next morning, a farmer sees him. He breaks the ice with a stick and frees the little duckling.

"Go and find your friends," says the farmer.

"I have no friends," says the little duckling sadly. He spends the long, cold Winter all alone.

At last Spring arrives. The days are warmer and there is plenty to eat. The wild ducks and geese come back to the lake. They have so many things to tell each other. But no one speaks to the little duckling.

The little duckling tries stretching his wings. He starts to flap them, and then he flies for the first time. Up he goes into the clear, blue sky. He should feel happy, but he is not. He looks down and sees some swans swimming on a pond. He decides to fly down and talk to them.

21

The little duckling settles on the pond. He says to the swans, "Please help me. I am so ugly and lonely. I have no friends." The swans are very surprised. "Have you looked at yourself in the water?" says one.
The ugly duckling takes a look at himself. What a surprise he has!

"Is that really me?" he asks.
"Of course it is," say the swans.
"You are a swan. All swans are beautiful."
Three children come running to the pond. "A new swan!" they say. "Please stay with us."
The ugly duckling has changed into a beautiful swan over the long Winter months. Now he will never be lonely again.

Can you find five differences between these two pictures?

Can you say these words and tell the story by yourself?

ugly duckling

wild duck

farmer

swan

Little Red Riding Hood

Little Red Riding Hood's mother is packing a basket with food. "Please take this to Grandma," she says to Little Red Riding Hood. "She is not well."
Little Red Riding Hood puts on her red cape with the red hood. Her mother waves goodbye. "Do not talk to strangers," she calls.

31

As Little Red Riding Hood walks through the forest, she sees lots of flowers. She decides to pick some for Grandma.

"Good morning," says a voice. It is a wolf. He looks inside the basket. "Where are you taking this food?" he asks.

Little Red Riding Hood forgets what her mother has told her. "I am taking it to Grandma. She lives in a cottage in the middle of the wood."

The wolf runs straight to Grandma's house and knocks on the door.

"Who is it?" asks Grandma.

"It is Little Red Riding Hood," says the wolf, in a high voice.

Grandma screams when she sees the wolf. He looks very hungry. Grandma jumps out of bed and locks herself in a cupboard. She drops her frilly bed-cap on the floor. The wolf puts on the bed-cap and pushes his ears inside. Then he climbs into Grandma's bed and pulls up the covers. He waits for Little Red Riding Hood.

Soon there is a knock at the door. "Who is it?" calls the wolf. He tries to sound like Grandma.

"It is Little Red Riding Hood," says Little Red Riding Hood.

"Lift up the latch and come in," calls the wolf.

Little Red Riding Hood goes in and sits on the bed. The wolf says, "What is in the basket?" As he leans forward, one of his ears pops out of the bed-cap!

39

"What big ears you have!" says Little Red Riding Hood.

"All the better to hear you with, my dear," says the wolf.

"What big eyes you have!" says Little Red Riding Hood.

"All the better to see you with," says the wolf with a grin.

"What big teeth you have!" says Little Red Riding Hood.

"All the better to EAT you with!" cries the wolf. He throws off the covers and jumps out of bed.

"You are not my Grandma!" cries Little Red Riding Hood.

"I am the big, bad wolf," says the wolf in his own voice. "And I am very hungry!" The wolf chases Little Red Riding Hood around the cottage.

43

Little Red Riding Hood runs out of the cottage. "Help! Help!" she screams. The wolf chases her into the wood. A woodcutter hears Little Red Riding Hood's screams. He sees her running away from the wolf. As soon as the wolf sees the woodcutter, he stops chasing Little Red Riding Hood and runs away.

Little Red Riding Hood and the woodcutter go back to the cottage. They hear Grandma calling from inside the cupboard. When Grandma is certain that Little Red Riding Hood is there, she opens the door.

"I will never talk to strangers again," says Little Red Riding Hood. "What a lucky escape we have had!"

Can you find five differences between these two pictures?

Can you say these words and tell the story by yourself?

Wolf

Grandma

Little Red Riding Hood

Woodcutter

The Three Little Pigs

The three little pigs live with their mother. One day she says to them, "Now you are old enough to go into the world and build your own homes."
The three little pigs are very excited. They wave goodbye to each other as they set off.

The first little pig builds his house with straw. It is not very strong. One day, the big, bad wolf knocks on the door. He says, "Open the door, little pig, and let me come in." He wants to eat the little pig for his dinner.

The first little pig says, "Not by the hair on my chinny chin chin will I open the door and let you come in."

"Then I will huff and puff and blow your house down," says the wolf. And he huffs and puffs until the house of straw is blown away. That is the end of the first little pig.

The second little pig builds his house with sticks. It is not very strong. One day, the big, bad wolf knocks on the door. He says, "Open the door, little pig, and let me come in." He wants to eat the little pig for his dinner.

The second little pig says, "Not by the hair on my chinny chin chin will I open the door and let you come in."

"Then I will huff and puff and blow your house down," says the wolf. And he huffs and puffs until the house of sticks is blown away. That is the end of the second little pig.

The third little pig builds his house with bricks. It is snug and warm and very strong. One day, the big, bad wolf knocks on the door. He says, "Open the door, little pig, and let me come in." He wants to eat the little pig for his dinner.

The third little pig says, "Not by the hair on my chinny chin chin will I open the door and let you come in."

"Then I will huff and puff and blow your house down," says the wolf. And he huffs and puffs until he is out of breath. The house of bricks does not move. It is too strong for the wolf to blow down.

The wolf is very angry. He decides to climb down the chimney. The little pig hears the wolf climbing onto the roof. "The big, bad wolf will never catch me," says the little pig. He puts a big pot filled with water over the fire. Soon the water is very hot.

The little pig hears the wolf climbing down the chimney. Suddenly there is a big splash. The wolf falls into the pot of hot water. And that is the end of him. The third little pig lives happily ever after.

Can you find five differences between these two pictures?

Can you say these words and tell the story by yourself?

wolf

bricks

straw

sticks

Aladdin

An old Chinese magician is looking for a magic lamp. He knows it is in a cave. The way into the cave is down a long tunnel. The magician is afraid to go into the tunnel because anyone who touches its walls will die. The magician decides to ask a boy named Aladdin to go down the tunnel and get the lamp for him.

The magician gives Aladdin
a magic ring to wear. "It will keep
you safe," he says.
"Safe from what?" asks Aladdin,
but the magician does not tell
him. Aladdin is gone for a long
time. The magician thinks he is
dead. At last the magician sees
Aladdin coming back.
"Give me the lamp," he says.
"Help me out first," says Aladdin.

The magician is angry. "If you will not give me the lamp, you can stay there forever!" The magician says a magic spell. The entrance to the tunnel is covered with a big rock. Aladdin is trapped. By chance, he rubs the ring on his finger. Suddenly a genie appears and says, "I am the genie of the ring. Your wish is my command." "Take me home," says Aladdin.

Suddenly Aladdin is back home. He is still holding the lamp. His mother decides to clean the lamp. She rubs it with a cloth. Another genie appears. Aladdin's mother is afraid. Aladdin asks the genie, "Who are you?"

The genie says, "I am the genie of the lamp. Your wish is my command."

Aladdin asks for money and a palace to live in. The genie makes Aladdin very rich. Aladdin even marries a princess. One day, the princess hears an old man outside calling, "New lamps for old!"

"I will change Aladdin's old lamp for a new one," says the princess. Aladdin has not told her that his lamp is magic.

The princess gives the lamp to the old man. Suddenly he throws off his coat. It is the magician. "Everything that Aladdin has will be mine," says the magician. He rubs the magic lamp, and the genie appears.

"What is your command?" asks the genie of the lamp.

"Take the princess, myself and this palace to Africa," says the magician.

When Aladdin returns home,
he rubs the ring on his finger.
The genie of the ring appears.
"Bring back the princess and
my palace," says Aladdin.
"Only the genie of the lamp
can do that," says the genie.
The genie takes Aladdin to the
princess instead.
"The magician has the lamp up
his sleeve," says the princess.
"Put this sleeping powder in
his drink," says Aladdin.

When the magician falls asleep, Aladdin takes the lamp from his sleeve. Aladdin rubs the lamp, and the genie appears.

"Take the palace and everyone in it back to China," says Aladdin. "But leave the magician here."

The genie does as Aladdin asks.

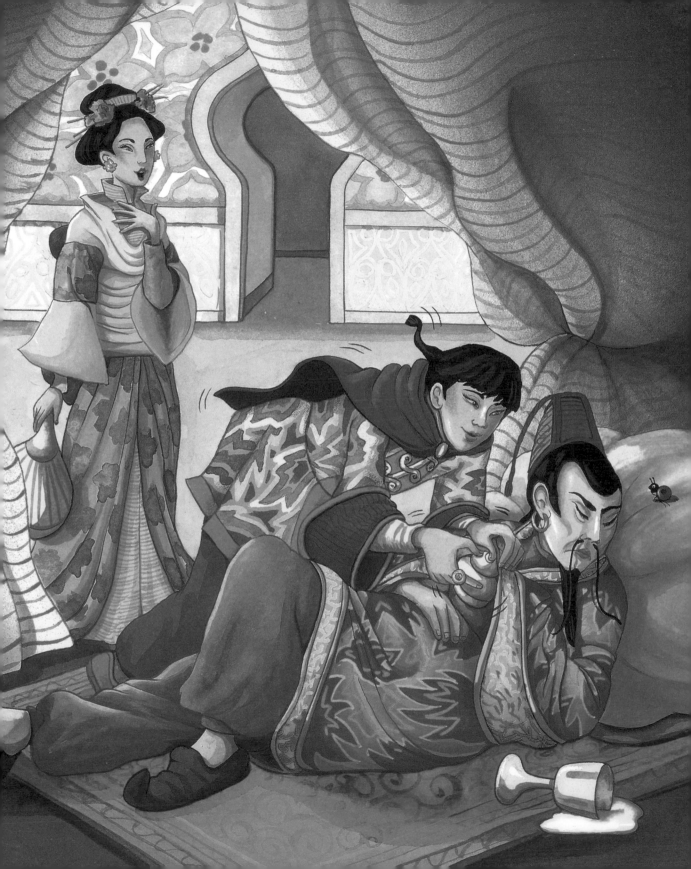

When the magician wakes up, the princess and the palace have disappeared. He looks up his sleeve for the lamp. It is gone, too. The magician never returns to China. Aladdin and the princess live happily ever after.

Can you find five differences between these two pictures?

Can you say these words and tell the story by yourself?

Aladdin

lamp

genie of the lamp

princess